The Cats' Wedding

First published in the United States by
Ideals Publishing Corporation,
Nashville, Tennessee 37214

by arrangement with Michael O'Mara Books, London

Library of Congress Cataloging-in-Publication Data

Smith, Linda Jane, 1962–
    The cats' wedding. / by Linda Jane Smith.
        p.   cm.
    Summary: An elegant house cat and a tough alley cat overcome the
gulf between their stations in life and get married.
    ISBN 0-8249-8402-1
    [1. Cats—Fiction]   I. Title
PZ7.S6543Cat   1989
[E]—dc19
                                      89-7422
                                        CIP
                                        AC

10 9 8 7 6 5 4 3 2 1

Printed and bound in Spain
by Graficas Estella, S.A. Navarra

The Cats' Wedding

Linda Jane Smith

IDEALS CHILDREN'S BOOKS
Nashville, Tennessee

Meet Suki Cat. Suki sleeps on a smooth silk pillow in a warm and comfortable house. Suki's Papa spoils and pampers her. She is a very contented cat.

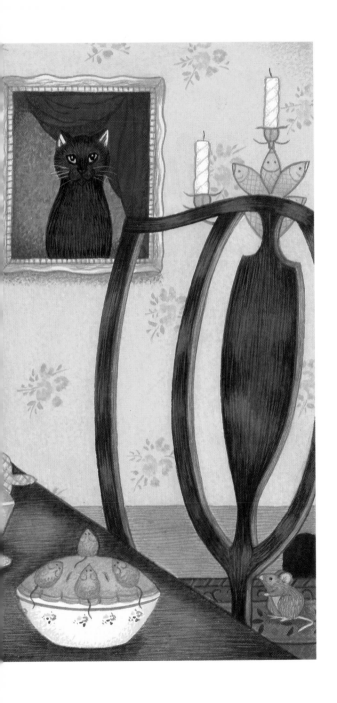

Portraits of the family's ancestors line the walls of Suki's home. Suki's Papa says, "We can trace our family line all the way back to Noah's Ark!"

Dinners are large and delicious in Suki's house. Her Mama often broils a large tuna or fries chicken for Sunday dinner. Suki's favorite dessert is a dish of warm cream.

7

Meet Barney the alley cat. Barney's bed is a cardboard box with an old blanket for a cover.

Barney must go out each day and hunt for his dinner of scraps or fish heads. Poor Barney!

9

10

Barney has a huge family. He has ten brothers and sisters and more cousins than he can count. When Barney's dad was young, he was a fighter. He was the "alley cat champion" of the alley. Now Barney is recognized as the toughest cat on the block.

One day Barney decided to see the world beyond his alley. He said good-bye to his dad. He said good-bye to his friends. Then Barney set off to see what lay beyond the block.

It was a beautiful day and there were so many things to see that Barney prowled further and further from home.

When he came to Suki's yard, however, he just stopped and stared. There was Suki, sunning herself on the porch swing in the late afternoon sun.

Barney introduced himself to Suki. They talked and laughed and had such a good time that Barney asked if he could call on her. Suki thought that Barney was very handsome and very nice. Barney thought Suki was smart and very beautiful.

17

18

One evening Barney and Suki went to a very special restaurant. After dinner Barney took Suki's paw in his and said, "Suki, you have become very special to me. I want you to share my life."

"Oh, Barney," sighed Suki, "I want us to have a life together, too, but I don't know what Papa will say. He still treats me like his little kitten, and I don't want to hurt him."

"Leave him to me, Suki," said Barney.

The next evening, Barney knocked on Suki's door and asked to see her Papa. For the first time in his life, Barney was frightened. He was a tough cat in the alley, but he felt very little as he entered the den and stood in front of Suki's Papa. Suki's nosy little sisters were giggling behind their Papa's chair.

"Good evening, sir," said Barney. "I have come to ask for your daughter's hand in marriage."

"Which daughter?" replied Papa as the little sisters giggled.

"Why, Suki, of course," said Barney.

"You are too young," said Papa. "You have no way to feed my daughter."

"I will provide her with more than she can eat," insisted Barney. "I will give her anything she could possibly want."

"You will have to prove this to me!" shouted Papa.

"I will!" said Barney, and he dashed from the house.

21

Barney knew that Papa loved fresh mice. When he returned with
a tray full, Papa licked his lips. "Why don't you put those mice on

the table and we'll discuss the wedding after dinner?" he said.

After dinner Suki, Barney, and Suki's Papa and Mama planned the wedding. It was set for the following week. On the morning of the wedding, Papa turned to Barney. "You're welcome to use our guest bath, Barney," said Papa with his nose in the air.

Barney had never been in a bathtub before. He had always washed himself in the way cats have for centuries.

26

On the morning of the wedding, Suki sat before her mirror. While she brushed her fur, she said to herself, "I'm so glad I met Barney. We'll be so happy together. And I do hope everyone has a good time today," she purred. "I hope Barney's family feels at home, and I hope his Mom and Dad *like* me."

But Suki needn't have worried. Mom and Dad Alley-cat loved
her. The guests had a wonderful time, and they ate and drank

and danced until the sun came up. And everyone agreed that Suki
and Barney (as seen in their wedding photo) were just the
handsomest couple ever!

Cats everywhere are still talking about the wedding and the feast. There were lobster and mouse and fish-tail sandwiches –

everything a cat could possibly want. There were several
speeches and, later, a great deal of singing.

By that time, Mr. and Mrs. Barney Alley-cat
had gone off on their honeymoon.